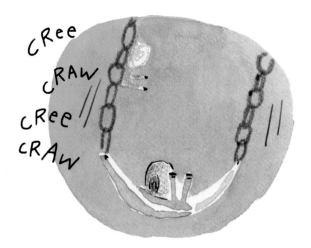

About This Book
The illustrations for this book were done in India Ink, Japanese watercolor, pastel, and colored pencil on Fabriano Artistico watercolor paper. This book was edited by Alvina Ling and designed by Brenda E. Angelilli. The production was supervised by Patricia Alvarado, and the production editor was Annie McDonnell. The text was set in YWFT Absent Grotesque, and the display type was hand drawn.

Sorry, Snail

Tracy Subisak

Little, Brown and Company
New York Boston

Ari was mad.

She was not allowed to yell
when upset, so she danced.

Wiggle here.

Jiggle there.

Until she heard . . .

munch
munch
munch

Ari stormed up to find . . .

Ari whispered wildly.

Look at that slimy body.

That silly shell.

Now this is when she got real, real close
and did the whisperiest of whispers.

Snail stopped munching
and zoomed away.

(At a snail's pace, that is.)

That night, as Ari fell asleep . . .

she heard the strangest sound.

Ari peeked her eyes open.

THAT SNAIL JUST SPOKE.

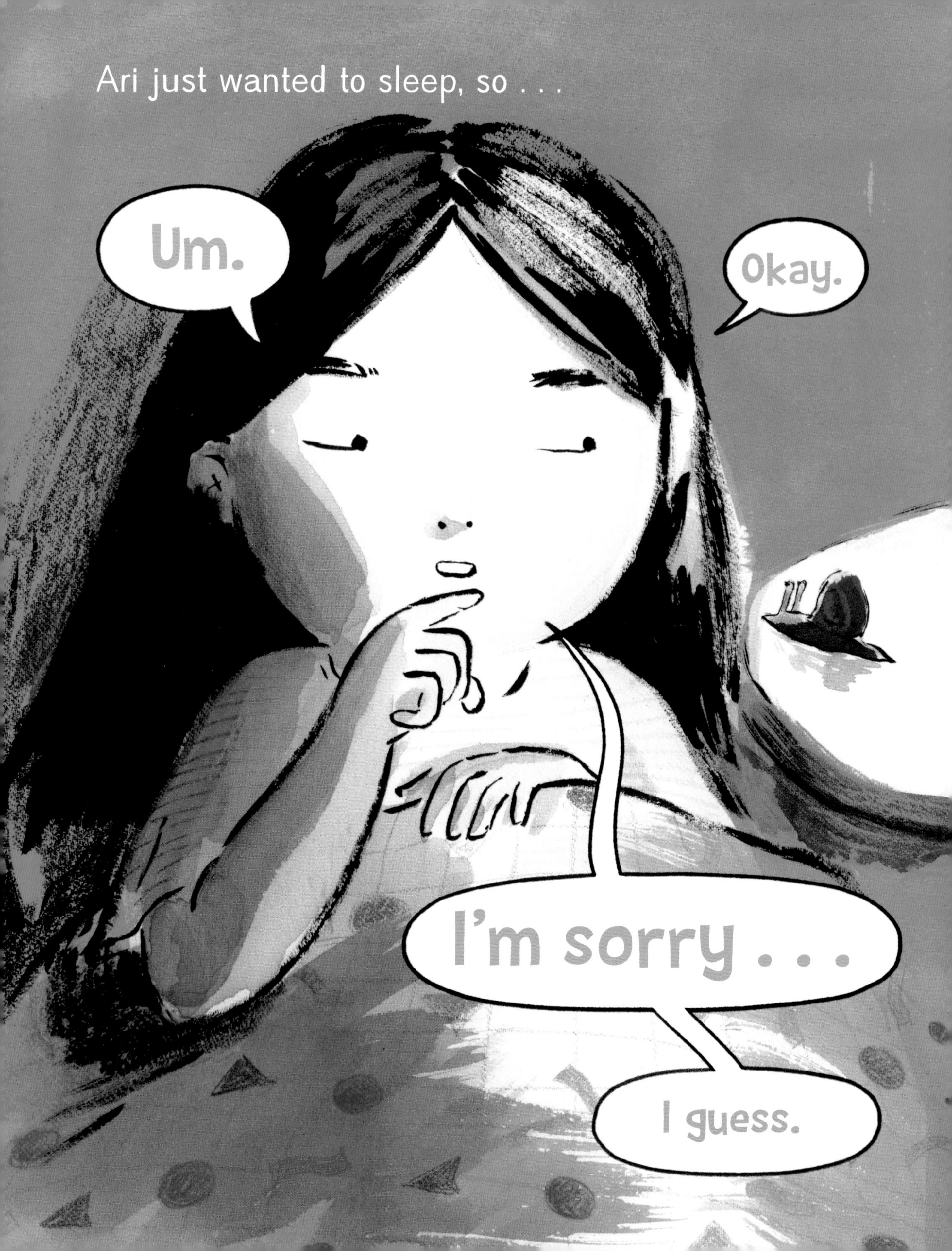
Ari just wanted to sleep, so . . .
Um.
Okay.
I'm sorry . . .
I guess.

Ms. Snail's eyes telescoped into Ari's soul.

Ms. Snail slunk away.
Leaving Ari frozen . . .
and very awake.

The next morning, Ari was greeted by . . .

MS. SNAIL.

Yikes! Ari quickly scooted past
Ms. Snail and to the playground.

Ari made her way to the monkey bars and encountered . . .

Blegh!

SLIME.

Hmph!

Ari looked up.

Ms. Snail!

AGAIN.

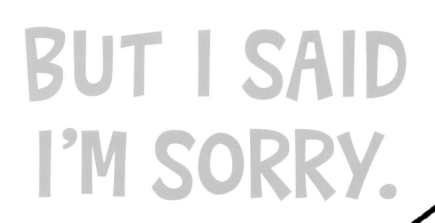

BUT I SAID I'M SORRY.

Ari yelled.

Ah, but you do not know that I saw into your soul, and it whispered to me, "I am not actually sorry."

Suddenly (or rather, slowly) hundreds of snails slid up from all the nooks and crannies to face Ari.

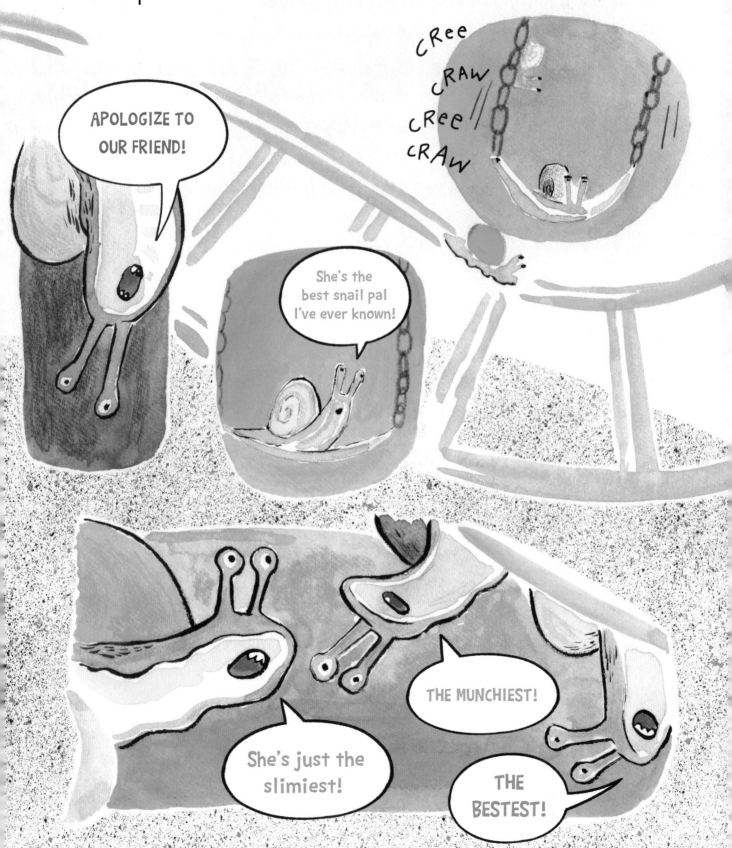

It is time for Snaily Justice!

yelled Ms. Snail.

Ari could feel the rage emanating from the escargatoire. The only thing she could do was run.

DARN TOOTIN'!

Yeah!

Huzzah!

Ari's day was ruined because of Ms. Snail and her friends' relentless behavior. She was feeling hurt.

Ms. Snail should really apologize, thought Ari.

She deserves an apology!

But then she was reminded of how she treated Ms. Snail in the first place.

Ari knew what she needed
to do. She pulled out her
chalk and got to work.

She finished the moment
the escargatoire reached her.

She scooped up Ms. Snail and lifted her high to see . . .

Ms. Snail— YOU ARE DELIGHTFULLY SLIMY!

Ari looked into Ms. Snail's soul, and
Ms. Snail looked into Ari's soul.

And they both knew they really meant it.

Ari liked to dance when she was happy.
And so did Ms. Snail.

So they wiggled and jiggled
all the way home.

Ari's night was just like any other. Except this time, she knew she had made a new friend.